HELLO KITTY

and friends

The Wedding Day

HarperCollins *Children's Books*

MEET HELLO KITTY
and friends

Hello Kitty

Mimmy

Tammy

Mama

Papa

Grandpa

Grandma

Fifi

Dear Daniel

With special thanks to
Linda Chapman and Michelle Misra

First published in Great Britain by HarperCollins *Children's Books* in 2013

www.harpercollins.co.uk
1 3 5 7 9 10 8 6 4 2
ISBN: 978-000-751441-0

Printed and bound in England by Clays Ltd, St Ives plc.

MIX
Paper from
responsible sources
FSC™ C007454

FSC™ is a non-profit international organisation established to promote
the responsible management of the world's forests. Products carrying the
FSC label are independently certified to assure consumers that they come
from forests that are managed to meet the social, economic and
ecological needs of present and future generations,
and other controlled sources.

Find out more about HarperCollins and the environment at
www.harpercollins.co.uk/green

Contents

Bridesmaids!

Hello Kitty did a little *twirl*, and her floaty pink dress spun out around her. It was made up of layers and layers of silky material and topped off with pretty netting – like a pink frothy milkshake! Hello Kitty felt like the perfect princess.

Hello Kitty smiled across the dressmaker's shop to where her twin sister, Mimmy, stood in exactly the same outfit, which was being worked on by the dressmaker. They were both going to be bridesmaids that very weekend and this was their last fitting. Hello Kitty looked around her – rolls of material, ribbons, and trimmings lay scattered around the shop. It was **messy**, but cosy, just as Hello Kitty liked it.

At that moment an older girl in her twenties came **running** in through the front door. It was their family friend, Emily, who the girls were going to be bridesmaids for. Hello Kitty's Mama and Papa had known Emily since she was a little girl. Emily had already had the fittings for her wedding dress, and she was here to pick it up, while taking a look at the bridesmaid's dresses too. Quickly, she called an apology to the dressmaker and hurried over to sit down with Mama.

Hello Kitty smiled. Emily was always late for everything!

Mama White crossed the room and straightened Hello Kitty's dress before **smiling** at both her daughters and putting a protective arm around Hello Kitty's shoulders.

Hello Kitty peeked a look at Mimmy. After the final fitting today they would actually get to take their dresses home! It was so **exciting!**

At that moment, the dressmaker stepped away from Mimmy, and Hello Kitty, Mama and Emily each let out a little squeal. Hello Kitty had known their dresses were beautiful, but seeing Mimmy in the finished dress, it was even more perfect than she remembered! The dresses were nearly the same as Emily's wedding dress, except they were pink instead of white. She looked at

Mimmy. The dress had little rosebuds running

all over it and there was a pretty pearl trim

around the neckline.

Instead of a long train

it had a frothy tulle

skirt, and while Emily

was wearing a lace veil that cascaded down her

back and a sparkly tiara, Hello Kitty and Mimmy

had bows with rosebuds on them too. Mimmy

did a quick spin. **Ta da!**

Hello Kitty didn't think

she had ever seen her

looking so pretty.

Emily let out a little cry of happiness, and told them that she would feel very special with them by her side. Then she pulled two little organza bags from her pocket and gave them to Hello Kitty and Mimmy.

Hello Kitty gave a **gasp** when she opened hers. There was a little silver heart-shaped locket inside. Mimmy had the same. Emily told them that they were thank-you presents for being such wonderful bridesmaids.

As Mama helped Hello Kitty

put hers on around her neck,

Emily helped Mimmy.

Then, Mimmy dashed back
into her changing room to
take off the dress,
as Emily pulled
something else
from her bag. A pile of photos.

As Hello Kitty looked at them, and over
at the bag where they had come from, she
saw the cutest little black and white kitten
staring back at her! It had four white socks and
sparkling green eyes.

Emily told them that it was her new kitten,
Coco. She was adorable but also rather
naughty. Emily had only got Coco last weekend

and although it wasn't perfect timing with the
wedding being so close, Coco had fitted in well.
Emily hadn't been able to resist the offer of a
new kitten, as she'd always wanted one!

Hello Kitty knew just how Emily had felt.
She and Mimmy **l♥ved** animals – all
shapes, all sizes!

Emily told Hello Kitty and Mimmy that
she would really have liked Coco to
come to the wedding, but Coco
was still very playful and always up
to mischief. She was going to have
to stay at home.

Emily took a deep breath

before asking them what they thought of their

bridesmaid's dresses.

Hello Kitty and Mimmy looked at each other.

There was only one answer to that...

Super!

Emily hugged them, then disappeared back

into the bridal shop to collect her own dress.

Hello Kitty looked at Mimmy, feeling little fizzes of excitement flutter through her. Two months ago they hadn't even known about the wedding and now it was just a few days away!

Mama told Hello Kitty that she needed to take her dress off too, so it could be packed up. Hello Kitty wanted to stay in it *all* day, but reluctantly she took it off and passed it over to the dressmaker's assistant. The assistant packaged the dresses up in tissue paper and put them in big carrier bags. As she reached over the counter to give them to the two girls, Mama asked Hello Kitty what the Friendship Club would think of the dresses.

The Friendship Club! Hello Kitty had nearly forgotten that they had a meeting that very afternoon! The Friendship Club was made up of her and her three friends — Tammy, Fifi and Dear Daniel. They met to do all sorts of fun

things likes arts and crafts, styling each other's clothes and dancing. They would all be there today – well, all apart from Dear Daniel, who was travelling with his dad.

Hello Kitty was sure that Tammy and Fifi would l♥ve the dresses. Not only that, but looking around the shop at all the materials had given her an idea for what they could do that afternoon.

Pushing back the door, Hello Kitty stepped out excitedly into the warm sunshine…

Just Make-believe

Tammy and Fifi squealed in *delight* as

Hello Kitty lifted the creamy pink bridesmaid's

dress out of its tissue paper, and held it up on

its hanger. It was later that afternoon and the

three friends were gathered at Fifi's house for

their Friendship Club meeting.

Hello Kitty smiled at her friends' reactions. She had known that they would l♥ve the dress as much as she did. As soon as she had been asked to be a bridesmaid she had told Fifi and Tammy all about it.

Tammy asked if they had had a chance to practise for the wedding yet and Hello Kitty explained that the dress rehearsal was tomorrow, ahead of the wedding on Saturday. It was going to be in Emily's parents' garden, just down the street from Hello Kitty's house, in a big marquee.

Fifi and Tammy thought that it all sounded
perfect. They wished that they could go too. It
sounded like it would be the loveliest wedding
ever! Hello Kitty wished that they could

go as well, but she said that there was no
reason that they couldn't play at weddings that
afternoon instead. It was the super-cool idea
that she'd had at the dressmaker!

She pulled a bag from behind her back. Fifi
rushed over and pulled out the collection of
things Hello Kitty had gathered for them.

Ribbons

Glittery material

Paper

Glue

Buttons and sequins

Hello Kitty had thought of everything they needed to create their very own **perfect** wedding! She had even got her mama's old net curtains to make the veils.

Tammy and Fifi giggled with excitement and clapped their hands. They couldn't think of **anything** they'd like to do more! They looked through everything and decided to use the sequins and cardboard to make tiaras and the paper for some pretty bunting they could hang up.

Quickly the girls got to work. Pulling out
the little table in Fifi's room they sat down, and
soon they were cutting and sticking and gluing
and pasting.

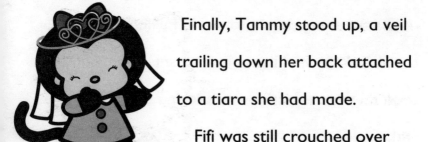

Finally, Tammy stood up, a veil trailing down her back attached to a tiara she had made.

Fifi was still crouched over a stack of paper. Folding it in concertinas, she had cut out *heart* shapes, *star* shapes and *diamond*-shapes before gluing sequins and sparkles on to them. Now she pulled them open and hung them from wall to wall. They looked great! Hello Kitty couldn't imagine that the real wedding decorations

30

could be any better.

Hello Kitty had been making a long skirt out of some more of the white net curtains. She wrapped it around Tammy's waist and then they both got the giggles as Tammy took her hand and solemnly marched her up a pretend aisle to a table. Fifi ran over to them with a couple of sparkly rings on a tray and a book in her hand. She gave each of them a ring and then told them they were now married, before collapsing in a heap of laughter.

At that moment, Fifi's mother came in with a tray of homemade lemonade and ginger-snap biscuits. She thought that the girls had all been working very hard and were in need in refreshment. They definitely were!

The three friends gulped down their drinks before collapsing on to the sofa. It was then that Fifi remembered that she had some **exciting news** of her own to tell them — she was going in an ice-skating competition on Friday! Hello Kitty and Tammy were as excited as she was! What was her routine like, they wanted to know?

So Fifi got up to show them – she spun and pirouetted across the floor, before finally coming to a standstill by Hello Kitty and Tammy.

Wow! They both cheered and clapped.

Fifi asked how she had looked, and her

friends told her that she had done brilliantly.

She would be sure to win. Now all Fifi needed…

was a promise that they would come and

watch! Tammy and Hello Kitty looked at each

other and winked – there was only one answer to that question. *Definitely!* The Friendship Club would be there!

A Very Cute Kitten

When Hello Kitty and Mimmy pushed back the

little gate to Emily's house the next day for

the wedding rehearsal, they couldn't believe

how pretty everything looked. The garden

had been completely transformed! White and

sparkling decorations and pretty pink bunting hung from tree to tree, and little fairy lights adorned the rose bushes. Right in the middle of it all stood the most amazing marquee they had ever seen. It was huge! Like a giant white meringue!

Emily hurried over to greet them, then led them inside the marquee.

Hello Kitty looked all around her. It was as *beautiful* inside as it was out. All of the tables had vases of summer roses on them and there was silver cutlery, folded napkins and confetti on the tablecloths as well as little silver bags of sweets. At the end of the marquee there was an arch of flowers where Emily would be married. Next to it there was a beautiful four-tiered

wedding cake with a little bride and groom

on top! Emily told them that it was fruit cake,

but that there would be a stand of chocolate

cupcakes for anyone who preferred them.

Delicious!

Hello Kitty was telling Emily how pretty everything looked but Emily didn't look quite sure. Whatever could be wrong? Hello Kitty asked her, and Emily admitted that while everything *was* beautiful, she had been hoping for **glitter** confetti to put on the tables but only plain confetti had arrived. Not only that, but Emily felt that there was something else that wasn't quite right with the inside of the

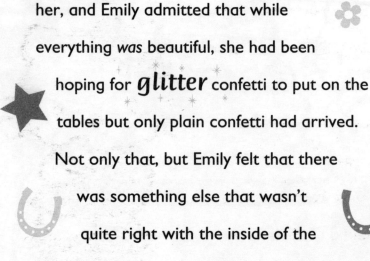

marquee. Could they guess

what it was?

Hello Kitty and Mimmy looked around.

They couldn't see what it could be.

Everything looked just perfect!

Emily asked them to look again, but still

Hello Kitty and Mimmy couldn't see a problem.

So Emily pointed to the

bunting. She bit her lip as

she told them that it was

pretty, but as it was just

plain old pink and white

she was worried that it

looked a bit dull.

It was hard to have a wedding and not worry about *everything* being just right!

Hello Kitty and Mimmy reassured her that it didn't look dull at all — it was really pretty.

It would have looked even prettier with a few more sequins and *sparkles* of course, but they didn't want to upset Emily by telling her

that. And besides, they didn't
have time to say any more
as at that moment, a little
black and white bundle of
fluff came bounding into the
marquee.

It was Coco! She was *sooo*
cute! Hello Kitty and Mimmy reached
down to give the fluffy little kitten a cuddle.

Emily **smiled** as she scolded Coco and
told her that she wasn't meant to be out
here, but it was clear that Emily
couldn't really be cross with the
kitten for long. She picked her up

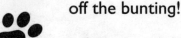

and hugged her. Emily told Hello Kitty and Mimmy that Coco was a bundle of mischief. The kitten had **already** chewed up some of the confetti and tried to pull off the bunting!

She put the kitten back on the ground. Coco mewed and then pounced on the hanging edge of a nearby tablecloth. Hello Kitty quickly scooped her up. She could see what Emily meant. Perhaps Coco was just a little bit too naughty to be allowed in the marquee!

Emily scooped Coco up and took her back inside, giving Hello Kitty and Mimmy the chance to look around the marquee a bit more.

There was a big dance floor set up at the end of it and little **twinkling** lights that hung from a black backdrop to give the impression of a night sky.

The girls thought it was going to be really good *fun* to dance there. They headed outside to where a man was halfway up a ladder, hanging fairy lights in the trees.

It was Emily's father, Mr Peters. He was older than Papa White and looked to be struggling a little bit as he reached across

between the trees. Every time, he

had to move the stepladder

a little to one side before

climbing up again. Hello Kitty

and Mimmy offered to help him

by holding the fairy lights whilst he

moved the ladder.

He was **delighted** to have their help.

Once they had finished, Mr Peters pointed

out all the tea light candles that Emily had left

for him to do something with. He wasn't sure

where they should go at all. But perhaps Hello

Kitty and Mimmy could help, he wondered

aloud, a small smile on his face.

The girls were very happy to help! Hello Kitty

suggested that they put them all around the

garden too – in the plant pots and along the path.

Mr Peters beamed at her. It was a great idea, although it was going to take him ages to do on his own… There were bags and bags of them.

Hello Kitty and Mimmy offered to help straightaway. It was so much **fun** setting up for a wedding! Mr Peters smiled again and thanked them.

They grabbed a bag and made a start. Once they had begun, Hello Kitty kept coming up with all sorts of different places as to where they could put the tea lights. It didn't take them long at all.

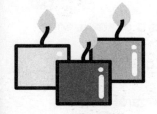

They had just finished when Emily appeared at the back door.

She looked worried as she told them that she had mislaid the tea light candles but when Hello Kitty and Mimmy told her that they had already put them out, she couldn't thank them enough.

Emily was *thrilled* with all of their help and declared to Hello Kitty that she should be a wedding planner when she was older.

Hello Kitty liked the sound of that!

Emily reminded them that it was time for the actual wedding rehearsal so, as everyone gathered in a group by the arch of flowers,

HELLO KITTY *and friends*

Hello Kitty and Mimmy took their places by the bride so they could run through how the day would go.

Everyone looked at each other happily as they quickly ran through their words and where they would need to stand.

As the practice run-through came to an end, Mama appeared at the gate to collect Mimmy and Hello Kitty. There would be **just enough** time for them to go

and see Fifi in her ice-skating competition that
afternoon.

Emily waved them off, telling them she
couldn't **wait** to see them again in the
morning – ready to get their hair and make-
up done. With Hello Kitty and Mimmy beside

her on the day, she was sure it would be the

best wedding day ever – nothing could

go wrong!

Oh no!

As Hello Kitty sat at the side of the ice-skating rink, in between Mimmy and Tammy, she pulled her red cardigan a little closer around her. It might be summer outside, but the cool from the ice was making her feel very **chilly**.

Mama patted Hello Kitty's arm and pulled a flask of hot chocolate from her bag. She handed a cup to each of the girls. It was almost Fifi's turn to skate! The previous skater headed off the ice and Fifi came gliding in. She stopped in the middle of the rink and waited for her music to start. Gracefully, she started skating round in a circle before turning and gliding backwards. She skated **faster** and

faster, and then she stuck one of her toes into the ice and leaped up into the air! She landed with one leg stretched out behind her and glided forwards.

Hello Kitty and Tammy gasped. Fifi was **amazing!**

They all clapped and cheered.

Fifi skated round again, on one leg this time, before she turned into a spin, leaning backwards, one hand holding her ankle. She spun round and round on the spot before stopping, then she moved forwards again. Jump followed jump as the music built up to the grand finale. She finished with a final spin, with her hands high above her head. *Wow!*

Hello Kitty and her friends cheered and clapped as loudly as they could. Fifi was beaming as she came off the ice and the next competitor went on.

Hello Kitty kept her fingers crossed as Fifi's scores were announced. She had got **really** good marks from all three judges! Everyone whooped in delight. Surely she would win?! They would know at the end when everyone else had finished skating.

Fifi had a massive grin on her face as she took her skates off and came over to her friends, enveloping them in a **great big bear hug**. Now all she could do was sit and wait.

Soon, the last skater came off the ice – the competition was at an end. They waited with bated breath as the results were announced in reverse order, from fourth place through to the winner. At last, at the very end, Fifi's name was called. She had done it! She had won!

Fifi skated forward on to the ice to collect

her prize – some flowers and a little silver cup. She curtsied gracefully, **Smiling** in delight. Once she came back off, Mama said that her win called for a special celebration and took them all off for ice-cream sundaes.

Hello Kitty didn't think she had ever felt happier as she looked around at her friends.

She and Mimmy filled them in on what they had done earlier in their day – from helping out with the marquee and meeting Coco, right through to the wedding rehearsal.

Tammy and Fifi thought that it sounded *amazing.* They definitely wished that they could go to the wedding the next day too!

As Hello Kitty and Mimmy snuggled into bed that evening, Mama pushed back the bedroom door. The twins had their own rooms, but on this special occasion, Mama had said that they

could share. She smiled and softly said that they

had to try and get some sleep, though; they'd

need to be bright-eyed for the next morning.

Hello Kitty and Mimmy assured her they

would – although they had no idea how they'd

ever get any sleep **at all!**

When they woke the next morning,

bright sunshine was already streaming in

through the bedroom curtains. Hello Kitty was

pleased to see that it was going to be a perfect

day for a wedding! They couldn't wait to get to

Emily's house.

Mama called out to them that they had to hold their horses, though. They had to have breakfast and clean their teeth first. It was no good going to a wedding on an empty stomach!

Finally they were ready, and waited by the door, clutching the bags with their dresses for Mama to come downstairs and take them the short distance to Emily's house.

As they walked down the street, Papa waved them off and called out that he would see them at the wedding.

Hello Kitty and Mimmy could hardly contain
themselves as they **skipped** and **jumped**
down the pavement, trying to walk carefully
with their dresses. How excited would Emily be?
What would she say? But when they pushed back
the gate and made their way into the garden,
they found something totally unexpected.

Emily was there ahead of them, but she was upset and a few tears were running down her cheeks.

What had happened?

Emily quickly told Hello Kitty and Mimmy that Coco had disappeared! Emily had looked everywhere for her, but the little black and white kitten was nowhere to be seen. Emily was very worried that Coco could have got out on to the street and she was about to go looking for her but at that moment, Emily's mother came out

of the house and told her that Coco couldn't

have gotten out – the gate had been closed the

whole time. That made Emily feel a little better,

but she was still worried about the little kitten.

Hello Kitty and Mimmy promised to look

for Coco while Emily carried on getting ready.

They started in the garden – looking under the

bushes and **UP** the trees before finally checking

 inside the marquee too, but Coco really was

nowhere to be seen!

 Hello Kitty felt awful. Poor Emily.

She was sure she would feel very

bad if she had a kitten and it had

got lost. **Especially** on her wedding

day! If only she and Mimmy could find Coco.

Where could she be? They had to keep looking!

But just then Mama called to them from the

house. There was no more time to search. They

had to get ready.

Still wishing they had

been able to find Coco,

Hello Kitty and

Mimmy went into the

house.

Mama took them

up to Emily's bedroom

where their dresses were

laid out on the bed. Emily's dress was hanging on the wardrobe door.

The make-up lady was just finishing Emily's make-up, so now it was Hello Kitty and Mimmy's turn!

Hello Kitty chose pale pink rosebud nail varnish whilst Mimmy chose *pretty* silver.

Hello Kitty fluttered her hands about in the air to dry them while Mimmy had her nails painted, and then they were allowed a little bit of lip gloss and some sparkly eyeshadow.

Their hair was brushed and then, finally, it was time for the girls to put on their dresses. Emily would get dressed in a minute, but she cooed over the girls in their bridesmaid's dresses. They looked the prettiest picture ever!

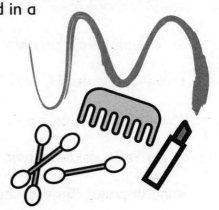

Emily's mother fetched the flower baskets that Hello Kitty and Mimmy would be carrying. They were filled with **bright** pink pansies and tiny rosebuds and little blue forget-me-nots.

Hello Kitty was admiring the different flowers when Emily asked her and Mimmy if they would mind popping down to the marquee to fetch her

purse, which she had left by the entrance. She

hoped it would be OK, she said – she would go

herself, but she needed to get dressed!

Hello Kitty and Mimmy didn't mind at all!

They loved helping Emily. Quickly, they went

down the stairs and outside into the sunshine.

Everyone was *really* busy, hurrying about

getting things ready for the wedding.

They ran down the little path and into the

marquee.

But... **Oh no!** Hello Kitty and Mimmy

both gasped as they saw the sight before them.

Something really terrible had happened!

The table decorations had been knocked

over, the confetti was

scattered on the

floor and the

bunting had

been pulled

down, some of it in rags. What on **earth**

had been going on?

Hello Kitty looked at Mimmy with her eyes

wide. Whatever had happened? With all of the

wedding decorations destroyed, the wedding

was going to be a **disaster!**

Saving the Day!

Hello Kitty and Mimmy didn't want Emily to see the marquee in such a mess, so they started running around, picking things up. As Hello Kitty collected the pink and white bunting, she noticed little scratches through the material.

They looked like claws marks.
Hmmm... They must have
been caused by Coco the kitten!
But right now it didn't matter how
the damage had been caused. What
mattered was fixing it!

Mimmy turned to Hello Kitty and asked
what they were going to do. Everyone else in
the house was busy, and they were never going
to be able to tidy the whole mess on their own.

Hello Kitty thought hard, and then
brightened. She might have an answer...
Who better to call on in a crisis than the
Friendship Club?

Hello Kitty rushed back into the house and

borrowed the phone. Quickly, she called Tammy

and told her what had happened. Tammy

promised that she would call Fifi and that they

would be there as fast as they could!

Hello Kitty and Mimmy carried on tidying the

marquee, all the time looking at their watches, as the time until the wedding started ticked away. If **only** Fifi and Tammy would hurry!

Just then, they heard a noise at the door. Fifi and Tammy had arrived! And they had brought all the spare bunting they'd made the other day when they were playing weddings, and all the spare materials and glittery paper too. **Phew**. Perfect!

Quickly, the four friends set to work,

putting up the bunting they had made before,

and speedily making some more.

Then Hello Kitty had an idea. Why didn't

they make some *glitter* hearts for the top

table too? Emily would love them!

They all looked at each other and agreed
that it was a brilliant idea! They

would start straightaway. They were

concentrating really hard as they set

to work. So hard that they didn't

hear the little sounds coming from

somewhere outside the marquee.

But, as they were just finishing,

they all heard a little mew. They

looked up. Coco! It had to be!

But *where* was she?

Hello Kitty followed the sound. She made her way through the marquee, looking all around, before **finally** she came to stand beside an upside down flowerpot.

Mew! There it was again!

Hello Kitty lifted up the pot and there underneath was Coco, looking a little sheepish, but pleased to be out. Just *wait* until they told Emily!

Hello Kitty and Mimmy ran into the house with the torn bunting and the little black and white kitten.

Emily was over the moon when she saw her kitten, but when she saw the torn bunting her face fell.

Hello Kitty and Mimmy quickly explained what had happened. But don't worry, they said – they had fixed **everything!**

Emily couldn't quite believe that they had managed to fix it all on their own. So Hello Kitty and Mimmy each took one of her hands, and pulled her down to the marquee.

There was an anxious moment as Emily looked

around at what the Friendship Club had done.

Would she like it? Was it OK? But then she

beamed.

Emily didn't just like it – she **l♥ved** it!

In fact, she thought it was even better than

before! **Hurrah!**

Fifi and Tammy were still inside, hanging up the

final few decorations, so Hello Kitty told Emily

who they were and how they had helped out.

Emily was so grateful for all

their help, and gave them the

biggest **smile** ever. And

as a reward, she said that

they must come to the

wedding too!

Fifi and Tammy couldn't

believe their luck. There would

be just enough time for them to run home and

change!

Hello Kitty was still holding Coco, but she

held her out to Emily. Emily took her and buried

her head in Coco's fur. She was such a naughty

little kitten! What could Emily do with her

while the wedding was going on? How could

she possibly keep her out of mischief? Hello

Kitty smiled. She thought she might just have a

SUPER idea...

The Wedding Begins...

As Emily walked down the aisle on her

father's arm, Hello Kitty beamed at the crowd

from her place behind her, holding the train of

her dress. Everything looked perfect, and Emily

looked beautiful! Hello Kitty grinned across at

her friends as she made her way down the aisle between the rows of chairs. Tammy and Fifi were sitting with Mama and Papa. Hello Kitty and Mimmy laid down the train as Emily came to stand beneath the arch of flowers, ready to get married.

Hello Kitty smoothed out her own dress and **grinned** even more as she glanced down at the basket she had

placed at her side. There was an extra-special bridesmaid with them — Coco the kitten! Coco popped her head out of the flower basket at that moment, a **glittery** bow around her neck. Everybody laughed, and even Emily gave a little giggle.

Afterwards, when the ceremony was finished, everyone gathered in the garden to drink pink fizzy drinks. There were special drinks for the girls. **Yum!** Strawberry Surprise Fizz, made out of fresh strawberries and sugar. Hello

Kitty didn't think she had ever
tasted anything so delicious.
She looked around her —
the garden was the most
beautiful place she had ever
seen as family and friends stood
in shining sunlight in their best clothes.

As the afternoon shadows lengthened
over the grass, and the fairy lights started
twinkling, it was time for them to go back
inside the marquee for supper. Hello Kitty put
Coco back in her flower basket where she fell
fast asleep, exhausted from the day.

After a delicious supper followed by wedding

cake, it was time for speeches. And just as the speeches were almost finished, Emily stood up to speak too. There were a few extra special people she wanted to thank herself – Hello Kitty, Mimmy and their friends! Quickly, Emily

explained to everyone what had happened – how her little kitten Coco had pulled down the decorations, but that Hello Kitty and Mimmy and their friends had stepped in and **saved the day!** Everyone stood up and clapped and cheered. Hello Kitty didn't think she had ever felt so proud.

She **smiled** at her friends. She knew she couldn't have done it without them. Good friends like them were always there to help.

In fact, Tammy thought that they should have another Friendship Club rule to add to their book.

Good friends are always there when you need them most!

Hello Kitty, Mimmy and Fifi agreed that it
was just right. Just then, the band struck up
to play for the first dance. Hello Kitty thought
Emily and her new husband made a lovely
couple as they walked on to the floor. After
a few moments of dancing on their own, they
gestured for everyone else to join them.

The Friendship Club couldn't wait to get up!

Hello Kitty and her friends danced and laughed, celebrating the night away on the dance floor. The marquee was **twinkling** with fairy lights, everyone was smiling and the music was ringing out. It was the perfect end to a perfect day. What could be better than that?

The end

Turn over the page for activities and
fun things that you can do with your
friends – just like Hello Kitty!

Party Decorations

Hello Kitty loves to celebrate, and celebrating means a party! And every party needs decorations. Check out Hello Kitty's ideas on the next pages, and you'll have the prettiest party around.

Quick Planning Tips

The first step of having a party is making sure you ask a grown-up if it's OK. Once you have permission, it's time to plan away! Pick where you want to have it, and then invite your friends. (Not too many!) You need to pick what you will do, your music, and if you need snacks and drinks. Ask your Mama or Papa if you will need to buy anything!

You will need:

- Coloured paper
- Scissors
- Long pieces of ribbon or string
- A hole punch
- Glue
- Tape
- Coloured pencils and other things for decorating – like glitter or sequins!

Confetti

Confetti is easy. All you need to do is use the hole punch on the coloured paper, to make lots of little round pieces of coloured paper. Gather it all together in a bowl or jar, and it's ready for throwing at the party. Make sure you tidy it all up when you're done!

Decorations to make

Paper Chains

Cut out lots of strips of different coloured paper, about 15cm long and 2 cm wide each. Glue or tape one together to make a ring, and then just keep going with the rest – making sure you link each one through the one before to make a chain, before you stick it! Hang them up to brighten up the room.

ALWAYS ASK A GROWN-UP FOR HELP BEFORE USING SCISSORS!

Bunting

You will need coloured paper, a long string or ribbon, and tape or glue. Cut out lots of big triangles from the paper and stick them, point downwards, along the ribbon or string. You can draw any design you like, or add sparkles! Then hang them from two points around the room.

Themes

Having a theme can make your party even more fun, and help you decide what sort of colours and decorations you want in the first place. Take a look at this list below, and pick one you like!

1. Rainbows – lots of colours!

2. Karaoke – sing along!

3. Winter Wonderland – nice and sparkly.

4. Movie Premier – dress up like your favourite stars.

5. Disco Ball – dance the night away!

Can you come up with any more ideas?

You'll need something delicious to eat at your party. Fruit kebabs are easy to make, healthy, and super-yummy too!

You will need:

Wooden skewers, and four different types of fruit.

Some that are good are:

Apples

Bananas

Strawberries

Grapes

Starfruit

Pineapple

(fresh or tinned)

Clementines

Mango

MAKE SURE YOU ASK MAMA OR PAPA TO HELP!

★ ★ ★

1. Wash your fruit, and peel it if you need to!

2. Carefully cut or separate your fruit into chunky pieces.

3. Thread the pieces on to a wooden skewer – try lots of different colours until each one is full.

4. Cover them on a plate, and put them in the fridge for at least half an hour.

HELLO KITTY TIP

Hello Kitty

These can be even more yummy when you dip them in something too! You can try yoghurt, honey, chocolate syrup, or even hundreds and thousands!

Turn the page for a sneak peek at

HELLO KITTY *and friends'*

next adventure...

The Beach Holiday

Hello Kitty skipped around the kitchen table putting out her favourite pink stripy plates. She was excited because her friends Tammy and Fifi were coming over to her house for a Friendship Club meeting! The three girls and Dear Daniel had started the Friendship Club a little while ago. They held meetings, went on trips out and made up rules about being a good friend. It was really great fun!

Hello Kitty folded some pink serviettes into triangles and put one neatly on each plate. She couldn't wait until the meeting – they had so much to talk about! A little while ago, Tammy's parents had invited them all to go away for three nights to a little holiday cottage which was next to a sandy beach. It would be the very first Friendship Club holiday – how exciting was that? Unfortunately, Dear Daniel couldn't go because he was travelling with his dad, but he had told them to have a great time and made them promise to tell him all about it when he got back. They were setting off to the cottage the very next day.

Hello Kitty arranged some freshly-baked chocolate chip cookies on to a plate. She had just made them! She fetched some lemonade and found pink straws for the cups.

Just then there was a knock at the front door. Hello Kitty raced to open it and found that Mama had beaten her to it – Fifi and Tammy were standing on the doorstep! The girls hugged and said hello and then all ran into the kitchen together.

Soon the three friends were sitting around the table, munching happily. The cookies were still warm and the chocolate slightly melted. Yum! Everyone wanted to talk about the holiday –

what they would do, where they would go, what they would pack. Hello Kitty opened her sparkly notepad and suggested that they made a list of all the things they might like to do while they were away. The others started to call things out...

Find out what happens next in...

Win Hello Kitty Goodies and prizes!

Collect the secret passwords in the first six Hello Kitty and Friends books, and go to **www.harpercollins.co.uk/HelloKittyandFriends** to download your exclusive Hello Kitty activities, games and fun!

Collect all six secret passwords to win super-special goodies!*

Coming soon: